W9-APV-180

MEGAN'S TREE

MEGAN'S TREE

TREE

AND OTHER FAVORITE STORIES
Compiled by the Editors
of
Highlights for Children

Compilation copyright © 1995 by Highlights for Children, Inc.
Contents copyright by Highlights for Children, Inc.
Published by Highlights for Children, Inc.
P.O. Box 18201
Columbus, Ohio 43218-0201
Printed in the United States of America

All rights reserved

ISBN 0-87534-654-5

Highlights˙ is a registered trademark of Highlights for Children, Inc.

CONTENTS

MEGAN'S TREE

By Margaret Springer

"Bye, Mom! I'm going to my tree." Megan slammed the apartment door, ran down the stairs, and hurried across the street to the new shopping mall.

The sun felt almost warm. Spring would be here soon. She half ran, half skipped along the edge of the parking lot.

Behind the mall in a far corner, on a small patch of vacant land, stood an old apple tree.

Long ago there had been farms where Megan lived, but now the farms were gone.

Megan ran the last few steps and leaped onto the old plastic swing. She pushed with her feet, up and down, up and down. She closed her eyes as she swung higher, smelling the fresh earth, listening to the sparrows chirping, feeling the cold wind in her hair.

"This is my special place," Megan said aloud.

No one else seemed to notice the old tree. Every spring it was covered with fragrant white blossoms. In summer it made dense shade. In fall it was loaded with red apples. In winter the bare branches made beautiful patterns against the sky.

Until last year. Last year the tree had not had many blossoms. The leaves, when they came, were thin and curled. There were only a few wormy apples. Last winter, the branches had seemed to sag sadly under the weight of the snow.

Megan got off the swing and looked closely at the gnarled trunk. "This year you'll have blossoms again," she whispered. But she noticed, farther along the trunk, a bright orange paint mark.

The sun was higher and warmer now. Cars went into the mall, and people hurried to and fro in the distance.

Suddenly, a truck engine buzzed on the air, getting louder as it came closer. A city works crew stopped next to Megan, and two workers in yellow hard hats jumped down. One of them carried a giant chain saw.

"Sorry, missy," said the man. "This tree's dead. We have to cut it down before it falls down and hurts someone."

"But this is a special tree! It has my swing in it!"

The second man shook his head. "It isn't safe," he said.

They took Megan's swing down, carefully, and handed it to her.

For a long time the chain saws clattered and shrieked and whined. Megan sat on the asphalt, burying her head in her knees, her eyes shut tight and her hands covering her ears.

When the noise stopped, she peeked over one arm. A smoky haze drifted upward. A pile of logs and branches lay where the tree had been. The men loaded them into their truck and drove off.

Megan tucked her swing under one arm and began to slowly walk home. At the garden center beside the mall, spring plants and seedlings were for sale.

"Do you have any extra apple trees?" Megan asked one of the salesclerks.

"Extra? Well, we have these on sale, just like the rest."

"I just thought—" Megan hesitated. "That tree behind the mall was cut down. I thought if you had an extra we could plant it back there."

The woman smiled. "Not a chance," she said. "They need that space for a bigger parking lot. It'll be paved over soon."

That week Megan was busy with friends and school. Sure enough, the next time she went to the mall, stripes of yellow paint marked new pavement and new parking spaces.

The plants were still on sale.

"Would anyone mind if we planted an apple tree here?" Megan asked Mom one evening.

"What, behind this apartment building? No way, Megan. There's just a tiny patch of scrubby grass, and it's shady, too. You couldn't put a tree there, even if we were allowed to."

That night Megan dreamed of the old tree, but it was a young tree in her dream. A farm family lived in a farmhouse. Animals were in the barn. Crops grew in the fields. And rows of neatly tended apple trees stood in the orchard, each one loaded with juicy, red apples.

She drew pictures when she woke up. She took them to school and told about her tree.

"That's progress," somebody said. "In a new area like this, these things happen."

"But I wanted to plant another tree somewhere else. I know old trees die, but we could plant new ones." Megan pointed out the school window. "Look," she said. "Over there by that old stone fence is a lot of mud. I bet there used to be a farm right where this school is."

She sat down, feeling dejected. Then she stood up again. "Hey! Maybe we could have an apple tree here!"

The others thought it was a great idea. Their teacher checked with the principal and with the other teachers. The custodian helped with plans.

The idea grew into a fenced-off garden area in the back corner of the playground. Kids and teachers planted shrubs and flowers. They sodded the area with green grass. In a special place, Megan helped plant a young apple tree.

"It will be a long time before kids can swing on this one," her teacher said. "By that time you'll be finished school, Megan."

Megan nodded. "That's OK," she said. "Other kids will enjoy it." She closed her eyes and sniffed. Spring had come at last. The air felt warm. "This is my new special place," Megan said.

The Habitat

By David Lubar

"Could I borrow a few of your tools, Dad?" Charles asked.

"Sure," his dad said, looking up from the bookcase he was making. "What do you need?"

Charles glanced at his list. "A saw, a hammer, nails, and I'll also need a piece of wood."

"Right over here." They walked to the wall. His dad took down a hammer and started to reach for a saw. "What kind of cuts are you making?"

"I just have to saw up a board."

His dad nodded. "This is the one you want. You know the safety rules, right?"

"Watch my fingers, take my time, don't force anything. Use my head."

"Good boy." He smiled and gave the tools to his son. "You know where the wood is. Take whatever you need. The nails are in those jars on the shelf."

"Thanks, Dad." Charles went to the pile of wood and looked for a good board. He found the one he needed right on top.

"What are you making?" his father asked.

"A habitat box. They showed us a film in school about how animals are running out of places to live," Charles said. In his mind, Charles had a picture of a wonderful habitat that some animal could use as a home or shelter. Humming, he started sawing. It was fun, and the fresh-cut wood smelled wonderful.

As Charles was about to saw the last piece, his older sister walked in. "Hey, what are you trying to make?" Nancy asked.

Charles explained what he was doing.

"It looks like you could use some help," Nancy said. "Your cuts aren't very straight, and you really should use a stronger joint."

Charles shook his head. It was his idea, and he wanted to do it himself. "No, thanks."

14

Nancy laughed. "Are you sure? Nothing's going to live in that mess."

Charles felt his face getting hot and red. He turned away from Nancy and started sawing the last piece. He was so angry that he almost got careless, but he caught himself in time. In a few minutes, he was wrapped up in his project again.

"Done," he finally said. He looked at the box. It was nothing like the picture in his mind, but it would have to do. He took it outside and searched for a good spot. There, in the back of the lawn, stood two oak trees and a small patch of wildflowers. "Perfect," he said. He put his box on the ground. For a moment, he just looked around at all the houses with their neat lawns. He'd never realized how few places there were for the animals.

Nancy came out and joined him. "Nothing would want to live in there," she said.

"Yes it would." Charles usually had fun with Nancy, but sometimes she teased him.

"Oh yeah? I'll tell you what; it something uses your habitat, I'll do your chores for a whole month. But if it doesn't, you have to do my chores for a month."

"How long do I have?"

"Three weeks?" Nancy suggested.

15

Charles nodded. He was sure something would use his habitat before then.

Every day Charles watched the box. But, even after two weeks, no animal had made a nest. A couple of squirrels had hopped past it, and one had gone inside to check things out, but nothing seemed to want to live there. He knew there had to be some way to make the box more inviting.

Charles went to the library to research the problem. He looked at all the wildlife books. He read so much that every time he closed his eyes he saw squirrels and rabbits and moles. Then it all clicked together. Charles almost shouted "Yahoo!" but he remembered in time that he was in a library.

For the rest of the week, whenever Nancy kidded him about the habitat, Charles just smiled.

"Nobody home," Nancy said, "Looks like no chores for me this month. Nice try, Charles, but your habitat is a flop."

Charles smiled again and walked out to his box. It was pretty crude, he realized. "Lift it," he said to his sister.

"What?"

"Pick it up."

Nancy shrugged. She lifted the box. Then she shouted and jumped back. "Yuck, it's crawling with bugs!"

"Yup," Charles agreed. "If you look closely, you'll probably find pill bugs, beetles, maybe some worms. All kinds of life. You said nothing would use my habitat box. It seems you were wrong."

"Bugs aren't animals," Nancy protested.

"I never said they were. I just agreed that if anything used my box you would do my chores. Isn't that right?"

Nancy looked as though she were about to argue, but she said, "You're right. I was wrong."

"I'll tell you what," Charles said. "I'll forget about the chores if you'll help me with one thing."

"What's that?" Nancy asked.

"I'd really like to make a birdhouse. I know exactly what things should look like in my mind, but I'm not good with tools. Would you help me?"

Nancy smiled. "OK. That would be fun. I like to build, but I never know what to make."

"Great." Charles headed toward the workshop with his sister. Already he was planning the wonderful birdhouse that they would make together.

Action Shot

By Marilyn Kratz

"What a boring place to spend our vacation," grumbled Kari, looking down from the second-story window at the dimly-lit street. "Why couldn't Grandma come to our place instead of our coming here?"

She opened the window wider. Not a breeze stirred in the quiet darkness of the small town nestled in the woods.

"I like it here," said Jake, her little brother. "Daddy and I are going to catch lots of fish in the river."

"But everyone else in my photography club is off to someplace interesting this summer," said Kari. "They'll get exciting photographs."

"You can take a picture of me with a big fish," offered Jake.

Kari lifted the damp bangs off her forehead. "Thanks, Jake," said Kari. "But I want to photograph something unusual."

"Maybe some unusual people will come into Grandma's basket shop downstairs," said Jake.

"They've all looked like ordinary tourists to me," said Kari. "They're nice, but—" She was interrupted by a rumble of thunder.

Jake drew back from the window. "Do you think it's going to storm, Kari?"

"I hope it does," said Kari. "Maybe it would cool off then." She started toward the stairs. "I'm going down to open the front door. We need more air up here."

Jake followed closely behind Kari. "Maybe we should keep it locked until Mom, Dad, and Grandma get home from Mrs. Carey's house," he said.

"I'll open it just a little," said Kari. "We won't turn on the lights, so no one will know the door is open."

Jake and Kari made their way slowly down the dark stairway that led from their grandmother's apartment to the shop below. The streetlight on the corner was too far away to provide anything but deep shadows. Kari cautiously led the way down the crowded aisles to the front door.

A flash of lightning lit up the shop just as Kari opened the door.

"Close the door! Hurry!" shouted Jake.

"It's only lightning," Kari comforted Jake. "There's a storm moving in. It has stirred up a little breeze."

"I wish Mom and Dad were here," said Jake, clinging to Kari.

"I just had a great idea!" said Kari. "I'm going to get my camera and take pictures of the storm." She hurried back through the dark shop with Jake clinging to her hand.

Upstairs, Kari lifted the camera from its case and checked the film.

She put the camera strap around her neck. "Come on, Jake."

A loud crash in the shop below made both children stop in their tracks.

"What was that?" cried Jake, his eyes wide.

"Shhh!" breathed Kari. "Something's in the shop!"

"What'll we do?" asked Jake, trembling.

Kari tried to think above the rapid pounding of her heart.

"I . . . I'll have to sneak down the stairs and out the back door to get help," she whispered. "You hide up here."

"No, I'm not staying here alone," whispered Jake.

"Come on," said Kari. "But don't make a sound."

A long rumble of thunder drowned out the shuffling sounds in the shop as they started down. Kari could hear the wind blowing stronger. The enclosed stairway was pitch dark, except for brief flashes of lightning.

The back door was only a few feet from the bottom of the stairs. Kari pushed Jake out into the alley. Then, just as she was about to dart out after him, an idea popped into her head.

She paused and turned back toward the dark shop. She had used her camera so often and so carefully in photography club that, even without being able to see, she could hold it steady and snap a picture now. The bright flash blurred her attempt to see what she had photographed, but she didn't wait for a second look.

"Run!" Kari yelled, pulling Jake along the alley and around the corner to the street. She looked up just in time to keep from running into Mom and Dad and Grandma

"Mom! Dad! I'm so glad you're here," cried Kari. Her knees shook as she gasped for breath.

"Whoa!" shouted Dad. "What are you two doing out here?"

"There's a burglar in the shop," cried Jake. "We heard him!"

"But the shop was locked!" exclaimed Grandma.

"Well . . . umm . . . I opened the door to let in a little fresh air," Kari admitted.

"And then we went back upstairs and Kari got her camera," Jake went on, jumping up and down in excitement. "And then we both ran out as fast as we could."

"Thank goodness you're safe," said Mom, hugging them to her.

"Stay here," said Dad. "I'll see what's going on in the shop."

As Dad started toward the shop, Jake shouted, "Look!" He pointed at a big buck with branching antlers, running down the otherwise deserted street. A flash of lightning revealed a basket hanging from one antler.

"There's your burglar!" said Dad, laughing.

"That deer?" Kari asked.

"It's happened before," said Grandma. "They come into town looking for handouts from the tourists. That one must have lost his way."

"No one will ever believe this back home," said Mom.

"Oh, yes, they will," said Kari, patting the camera hanging around her neck. "And I'll have a most unusual picture to show my photography club!"

The Toy Maker's Son

By Susan Cleaver

Once there was a toy maker's son named Gustin. He lived in his father's shop in a small, quiet village.

One day Gustin watched his father carve a horse from a piece of dried pine. He longed to be a toy maker, but what if he couldn't learn to make toys? He always seemed to make mistakes.

"Watch carefully," said Father. "Soon you'll be old enough to carve toys yourself."

"Yes, Father." Gustin tried to pay attention. But the wood shavings reminded him of snowflakes as they drifted onto the floor.

"Business has been slow lately," Father said as he finished the horse's mane. "If the customers won't come to us, we'll go to them."

Gustin and his father filled a sack with toys. They took turns carrying it through the streets of the village.

"Listen as I talk to the customers, Gustin, so you can learn to sell toys."

"I will, Father," Gustin promised.

By noon, they had visited five families, and the sack felt a little lighter.

The last family they visited had seven children. Father spread the toys out on the ground and told the parents all about them.

Gustin grew restless. Forgetting his promise to listen, he climbed into the empty sack. He pulled it up to his waist and jumped past Father.

The mother of the seven children said, "With all the toys here, your son is playing with the sack. That's what we'll buy "

Father rubbed his beard and frowned. He was not one to turn down a sale, so they carried the toys home in their arms.

That afternoon, Gustin and his father filled a

big wooden box with toys. They took turns carrying it through the streets to the village fair.

At the fair, music drifted lazily from wooden flutes. Villagers stood in line to buy apples and plums. The smell of cloves and cinnamon made Gustin's mouth water.

The only empty stall was rickety and cramped. They unpacked the toys. Often there were long waits between customers.

Gustin looked at the empty box. He thought it would make a perfect castle, so he drew towers and flags on it with a piece of charcoal.

A young boy came by, tugging on his mother's arm. "I want that castle," he said.

Father rubbed his beard and frowned.

Again Gustin and his father carried the toys home in their arms.

That evening, Father asked Gustin to clean up the scraps on his worktable. But they didn't look like scraps to Gustin. He made a stuffed sheep from a piece of wool. He used wood shavings for the stuffing and bits of leather for the ears and tail.

The bells on the door jangled as a man came into the shop.

The customer noticed the sheep. "This is very clever," he said. "Did you make this?" he asked Gustin. "I want to buy it!"

"Yes, sir," Gustin answered.

The man stopped in the doorway as he was leaving. He turned to Father. "You must be proud," he said. "Your son shows talent for making toys at such a young age." .

"But I just make things for fun," said Gustin.

"Things for fun, you say? That's what toys are!" the man responded.

The bells jangled again, and the man was gone.

Father rubbed his beard. Gustin noticed he wasn't frowning.

"Would you show me how you made that sheep?" asked Father.

"Watch carefully," said Gustin as he began to work. He looked up at the proud smile shining from behind the beard. Gustin knew it was the smile of a toy maker's father.

Hattie's Bathrobe Birthday

By Judy Cox

Hattie was famous for parties. Like the clown party she gave Kevin when he turned five, and the ballerina birthday she planned for her best friend, Jade. Even when she was small, she liked to play tea party with the little china tea set Grandma gave her. And now that she was ten, her whole family and all her friends counted on her to plan their parties.

But today, the usually efficient Hattie slammed the forks down on the counter. "Easy, punkin," said Dad. Hattie took a deep breath and tried to stay calm.

"We just can't have a party without Mom," Hattie told Dad as they cleared the breakfast dishes together. She frowned down at the dirty spoons in her hand. "Whoever heard of a birthday party without the birthday guest?"

"You know Mom has to work at the hospital on Saturday. She can't get home until midnight," Dad said as he rinsed off the plates and stacked them in the dishwasher.

"I know," muttered Hattie.

Monday she stayed in the classroom at recess instead of going outside to play. "Why the long face, Hattie?" asked Mrs. Wong.

"My mom's birthday is Saturday," said Hattie. "But she has to work until midnight."

"Have your party on Sunday instead," suggested Mrs. Wong. "In my family we often celebrate birthdays on a different day."

"I guess we could," said Hattie. "But in my family we usually have our party on the same day."

Jade didn't understand either. "In my family we don't even celebrate birthdays," she said.

"But in my family we always have a party with cake, decorations, and presents," sighed Hattie. "Only not this time."

On Friday, Mrs. Wong called on Hattie to give her book report. Hattie stood in front of the class. "My favorite story is Cinderella," she said, holding up a book of fairy tales. "When Cinderella goes to the ball, the fairy godmother warns her to leave at midnight . . . " Hattie stopped. Midnight!

Hattie stumbled through the rest of her book report. "What's up?" whispered Jade, as Hattie went back to her desk. "You look as if you've seen a ghost!"

"I think I figured something out," said Hattie.

She explained her plan to Dad as soon as she got home. "Sure," he said. "That's a wonderful idea! You figure out what you need and I'll get it. Don't forget to call Grandma and Grandpa. They'll want to come."

On Saturday Mom worked the long shift, so she was gone before Hattie got up. After breakfast, Hattie helped Dad bake a cake. She frosted it with dark blue frosting. She put white candles on the top and scattered silver candy balls across it like stars.

"Everything needs to be blue and silver," Hattie told Dad. "It needs to look like midnight."

"Everything?" he groaned. "I'll have to go to the store again. What else?" Hattie gave him her list. She wanted blue and silver balloons and silver paper for stars.

All day long Hattie worked. She and Dad ate dinner early. Then she headed for bed.

"Seven!" she complained. "Oh, Dad, do I have to? I'll never get to sleep this early!"

But Dad insisted. "You'll be up late tonight, punkin. I'll wake you when it's time."

Hattie lay in bed for a long time, listening to the TV in the living room. She finally fell asleep, thinking of Cinderella's mad dash down the palace steps.

It seemed like no time at all before Dad was saying, "Time to get up, punkin. It's almost midnight." Dad was wearing his plaid flannel bathrobe and smelled pleasantly of toothpaste and shaving cream.

Hattie yawned, got out of bed, and put on her red fuzzy bathrobe and bear paw slippers. She followed Dad into the living room.

The room looked dark and mysterious. The streetlight, shining through the window, made a pattern of white squares on the rug. Hattie thought of other special nights, like Halloween and Christmas Eve. Even after Dad switched on the lamp, Hattie felt excitement prickle the back of her neck.

Hattie decorated the table and walls with moons and stars cut from silver paper, while Dad hung bunches of blue and silver balloons from the ceiling. Finally, Hattie set the cake in the center of the table on Mom's best tablecloth.

The doorbell rang. Grandma and Grandpa! She ran to let them in. "Oh, goody! You both wore your bathrobes!"

"Of course! We couldn't miss one of our Hattie's famous parties. A midnight bathrobe birthday party. What a charming idea," said Grandma, giving Hattie a hug.

"Mom will be home soon. Let's turn off the lights now, so she'll be surprised."

Hattie crouched in the dark, the collar of her bathrobe stuffed in her mouth to keep from giggling. Would Mom be surprised? Or would she be angry to find Hattie up so late? Her heart pounded in her ears.

She heard Mom's keys in the lock and saw light shining through the doorway. "Surprise!" yelled Hattie, running to give her a kiss. "Happy birthday, Mom!"

"What a surprise! I didn't think that anyone would remember my birthday," said Mom. "What beautiful decorations! What a beautiful cake!" She hugged everyone.

After Mom opened her presents, everyone had a piece of cake. Then it was time for Grandma and Grandpa to leave, calling good night through the frosty air.

Mom came in to Hattie's room to tuck her in bed. "It was the best birthday party anyone's ever given me," she said, kissing Hattie.

"No one turned into a pumpkin at this midnight bash," Hattie said sleepily. She snuggled under her covers. Even Cinderella's fairy godmother couldn't top Hattie's famous Bathrobe Party.

Market Day

By Margaret Springer

Amos looked across the rows of stalls at the Farmer's Market. Smells of baked goods, coffee, scented candles, and spices wafted in the early morning air. Through the open door, he caught glimpses of sunshine and vendors outside, selling bunches of cut flowers, jugs of apple cider, baskets of fruit and vegetables.

He was proud that Father had trusted him, for the first time, to run the stall by himself. He and Mother had to stay home today and care for Grossmommy.

"I know you can do it, Amos," Father had said.

The crowds were large this morning, and it wasn't even eight o'clock yet. Amos yawned and watched the people going by—tourists and city folk, mostly, with lumpy baskets, bags, and packs. A boy his age, wearing a colorful T-shirt, shorts, and a baseball cap on backward was buying flowers. For a moment Amos wondered what it was like to live in the city.

"Our ways are different," Father always said. And Amos knew it was true. He adjusted his straw hat. It was all right to be different.

"I'll take this jar of apple butter, please," a voice said. Amos jerked his head back to his own stall. Another woman held out money for preserves. A man behind her wanted honey.

It was always that way at the market. People came in bunches or not at all.

Amos fumbled for change in the cash box. He counted carefully, to be sure he was right. He wanted Father to be proud of him.

A man was looking over the baked goods at one end of the stall. Every week Mother baked two dozen pies for market: raspberry, peach, shoofly, schnitz. They sold fast.

"What kind of pie is that?" the man asked.

"Shoofly," said Amos. "Molasses, mostly. It's wonderful good." He turned to sell more honey.

At last the rush was over. Sales were good today. Amos counted the money in the cash box. Then he reached for the envelope to count the wad of paper money. Amos kept it under the cash box, hidden near the back, behind the pies.

The envelope wasn't there.

Amos anxiously searched under the long trestle table and on the cement floor below. The envelope was gone.

Then Amos remembered the man who had asked about the pies. He had been picking them up, looking them over. And then he had suddenly disappeared into the crowd.

Amos felt cold. "You can count on me, Father," he had promised. And now someone had stolen the money.

Gradually, the crowd thinned out. Vendors began packing things away.

Sadly, Amos sorted the leftovers and carried them in boxes to Joseph Martin's stall. This stern old neighbor had brought Amos with him today in his buggy.

"I was just coming to fetch you. Are you ready?" Joseph Martin asked.

Amos hung his head.

They carried everything to the buggy shed, where the horses waited. Amos helped Joseph pack his empty bushel baskets and boxes securely into the back of the Martin buggy.

They were covering everything with an old blanket when Amos saw someone in the crowd. The man who had stolen his money. He was sure of it. The man was standing at the back of an old car, loading a big bag of potatoes into it.

Amos hesitated. He knew what city people would do. City people would call the police. But our ways are different, he reminded himself. Our people don't hold with such things.

Amos tried to think. What would Father do?

"I'll be back in a minute," Amos called.

He ducked between buggies and bushel baskets and hurried past boxes and crates outside the buggy shed. He ran down a row of cars and came to stand next to the man.

The man turned and noticed Amos. His face showed that he was the one.

Amos swallowed hard. "I—I think you forgot something," Amos said.

"What did I forget?"

"This." Amos held out the cash box. "If you wanted everything, you should've taken this, too."

The man's eyes widened. He opened the box enough to see it was full of coins. "You're—giving this to me?"

Amos knew his voice sounded shaky. "Maybe you need it," he said, shrugging. "People steal sometimes when they're hungry."

"Look, kid, I'm not—I'm not hungry." The man looked around uneasily. Suddenly he jerked the fat envelope from his pocket and thrust it, with the cash box, back into Amos's hands. "Here, I—take it, OK?"

"Amos!" The Martin buggy was pulling out into the lane

Amos ran to catch up. He clutched the envelope in one hand, and the coins jingled in the box in his other hand as he ran.

The man revved his car and took off toward the highway. Dust hung in the air.

Sheba, the Martins' horse, tossed her head.

"City people are always in a hurry," Joseph Martin sighed. He looked across at the fat money envelope in Amos's hands. "You did well this morning, Amos?"

"Yes," Amos said. They turned onto the highway and then to a side road. Fields, rolling farmland, and neat farmhouses stretched away into the hazy distance.

"Your father will be pleased."

Amos smiled a small smile. "And I'm pleased, too," he said quietly.

Grandpa's Slippers

By Ann Bixby Herold

The Christmas after Ally was born, there was a box under the tree with a card that said:

TO GRANDPA
FROM BABY ALLISON

In the box there was a pair of slippers.

"Thank you, Ally." Grandpa lifted her out of her cradle and kissed her. "Did Grandma tell you I needed a new pair? And how did you know carpet slippers are the kind I like best?"

Ally smiled and gurgled and waved her tiny fists.

"We went shopping together, didn't we, Ally?" said Grandma.

Grandpa gave Ally a soft, stuffed rabbit named Rupert.

When Ally was bigger, she always took Rupert when she went to her grandparents' house. And Grandpa always greeted them at the door wearing the slippers.

"Did I really buy them for you when I was a baby?" Ally would ask.

He nodded. "It was your first Christmas and you went shopping with your grandmother." Grandpa always looked sad when he said that, for Grandma had died when Ally was three.

When Ally was five years old, so was Rupert. And so were the slippers. Rupert was looking worn, but the slippers were worse. One sole had been glued back on. When he wasn't wearing them, Grandpa kept them by his favorite chair.

"Ready for when my feet feel cold," he told Ally. "They are the best present ever."

"Like Rupert," said Ally. "Why are they called carpet slippers?"

"I guess because they look like they're made out of bits of carpet."

Ally nodded. The thick, dark gray fabric did look like carpet.

That Christmas Ally gave Grandpa a drawing of Rupert. Grandpa gave her a stuffed dog that she named Barney.

Ally's Uncle Mike gave Grandpa a new pair of slippers. They were bright red, with zippers up the front.

"I saw you needed new ones, Dad," he said. "These will cheer you up on cold winter mornings."

"Very nice Thanks, Mike," Grandpa said. He wore them over the holiday, but the next time Ally saw him he was wearing his old pair.

When Ally stayed overnight at her grandfather's house, she loved to watch him shave. He squirted shaving cream all over his chin. Then he let her draw pictures in the cream with her finger. Sometimes she wrote ALLY and, letter by letter, Grand pa slowly shaved it off.

When a dollop of shaving cream fell on his foot one morning, Ally said, "Why don't you wear your new slippers, Grandpa?"

"I'll tell you a secret," he whispered. "The color is too bright. I don't care how old and worn these are, I like them best."

Shopping with Ally at the mall, her mother said, "I wonder why your grandfather never wears his new slippers."

"He doesn't like bright colors," said Ally

"Then let's buy him another pair for his birthday," Mother suggested. "Those old slippers are a disgrace."

There were no carpet slippers in the shoe store.

"Good," Mother said. "I think they are ugly and old-fashioned." She held up an expensive pair in brown leather with a fleecy lining. "I think he will love these."

"I hope so," said Ally.

On his birthday, Grandpa pronounced the new slippers a good fit. And he liked the color. But the next time Ally saw him, he was wearing his old ones again.

"Your big toe sticks out, Grandpa."

"I don't care."

"And the sole is flapping loose again. You could fall and hurt yourself. My best friend Caroline tripped over her sneaker lace and she twisted her ankle."

"Ally, you sound just like your grandmother." Grandpa gave her a hug.

At Christmas shopping time, Ally saw a pair of carpet slippers in a store.

"Will they fit him?" she asked her mother.

"These are size nine and he takes a ten," Mother said. "I'm not wasting any more money on slippers for your grandfather."

Mother bought him a sweater instead. Ally made him a Christmas tree out of ice-cream sticks and decorated it with sparkles.

The week before Christmas, Grandpa fell on some ice.

"I was wearing boots, so don't try to blame my slippers!" he told his family when they rushed to the hospital.

Ally had brought along Rupert and Barney for company while he was in the hospital.

"I was going to buy you that bear you liked at Benson's Department Store, Ally," he said as she tucked them into bed with him. "If I give you money, could you buy it yourself?"

The holiday was over before Ally and her mother had time to go to Benson's. The department store was crowded, for the sales were on. On their way to the toy department, they walked past the shoes. There, on a sale table, was a pair of carpet slippers.

Ally stopped in her tracks. "They say ten. That's Grandpa's size. I'm going to buy them."

"He won't wear them, Ally."

"Yes he will." She bit her lip. "But I only have enough money for the bear."

"It might be gone," said her mother.

The bear was there. It had a sale tag tied to one leg.

"How much? Do you think I can buy both?" Ally held her breath.

"Where is your bear, Ally?" Grandpa asked when they stopped at the hospital on the way home. "Were they all sold out?"

"May I borrow your wheelchair, Grandpa?"

"Whatever for?"

"Wait and see," said Ally.

Out in the hallway, she sat the bear in the wheelchair and put the carpet slippers on his feet.

"Look, Grandpa!" she called from the doorway. "This is Bumper the Bear wearing his new carpet slippers. They are much too big for him, so he wants to know if you'd like to wear them."

"Thanks, Bumper!" Grandpa cried. "Lucky we both like the same kind."

The next time Ally saw her grandfather he was wearing the new carpet slippers.

And the next time.

And the next. . . .

The
Mysterious
Science Project
Disaster

By Catherine Carmody

My sweaty hands trembled, smearing ink all over the note cards for my speech. For about the hundredth time, I checked every detail of my science project. It's a display showing how solar cells work.

Talking in front of a bunch of people always gives me the jitters, but today was even worse. When our science class studied energy problems, I, Matthew Ables, decided to become a scientist. But would I be a good one? This project would be my first big test.

Most of the other fifth-graders wandered around the gymnasium, chatting with friends. Even a dog, part of Chris Barry's project, trotted by a while ago. Nobody seemed as nervous as I.

I noticed Mr. Holcomb, our school's custodian, peek into the supply closet right next to my table.

"Matthew," Mr. Holcomb said, "what's wrong? Are you sick?"

"Not sick, just nervous about this speech. I wasn't even hungry at lunch. And that's weird!"

"Well, *I'm* still hungry," Mr. Holcomb said. "I thought I left my roast beef sandwich on the supply closet counter, but now I can't seem to find it. But, about that speech, Matthew. You worked hard on it, right?"

"Right."

"Then I know you'll do fine."

Mr. Holcomb seemed so sure! He convinced even me. When Mrs. Valencia, our teacher, introduced me as the first speaker, I charged right into my speech.

"My project shows how solar cells use the sun's energy to make electricity. This lamp represents the sun. When I push the switch . . . "

I stopped talking for a moment while I switched on the lamp in my display. Nothing happened! The light bulb stayed as gray as a foggy afternoon.

What a disaster, I thought, as I crawled under the table to check the electrical plug. I even changed the light bulb. Nothing would make the lamp light up.

"It's all right, Matthew," Mrs. Valencia said. "Explain your project without the light."

So I did. But it wasn't all right. I bet nothing like this ever happened to Marie Curie or Thomas Edison, not even when they were in fifth grade. When I finished speaking, my mixed-up feelings collided, happy against sad. I was happy the speech was over. Sad that my career as a scientist was over.

I tried to pay attention to Jennifer Alvarez's speech about the scientific method, but my mind kept sneaking back to the disaster. Why wouldn't that lamp go on? By the time Jennifer finished, I still hadn't discovered a single clue to the mystery.

When it was Chris Barry's turn, the second disaster happened. Chris's dog, Autumn, had simply disappeared. She was part of Chris's project on animal training.

"I saw Autumn looking out the door," Jennifer said. "That was about ten minutes before we started our speeches."

Chris groaned. "Oh, no. Autumn loves to chase sea gulls."

Everyone knew that the playground would be swarming with sea gulls. As soon as our lunch period was over, the sea gulls would swoop down and squabble over the crumbs that kids dropped.

Our classroom aide volunteered to search for Autumn on the playground. Chris had to start her speech without Autumn.

"I trained Autumn to turn lights on and off for my dad," Chris said. "Since Dad was hurt in an accident, he has to stay in bed. When I give Autumn the command, 'push the switch,' she turns the wall switch on or off with her paw."

A bright light shining in my face made me squint It was the lamp in my display! As I hurried to turn it off, part of Chris's speech echoed in my head, like a familiar rhyme: "Push the switch."

Of course it sounded familiar. "Push the switch" was in my speech, too. It was the last thing I'd said before disaster struck.

That's when the fog evaporated from my brain. I knew why my lamp hadn't gone on. And I knew where Autumn must be, but I needed Mr. Holcomb's help. He was wiping off tables at the cafeteria end of the auditorium. I slipped away from the class.

"Mr. Holcomb, is there a switch that turns the power to the wall outlets on and off?" I asked.

"Yes, it's in the closet," he said. "They're on a different circuit than the ceiling lights."

"I think Chris's dog is in the closet."

"Let's go look. The switch is behind the supply cabinets."

The closet door stood partway open. I tiptoed in and peered behind the cabinets. There sat Autumn, right next to the electrical switch. A soggy scrap of bread lay on the floor beside her.

Mr. Holcomb chuckled. "I hope you enjoyed my sandwich, Autumn."

Chris had just finished her speech when we led Autumn out of the closet.

"Autumn!" Chris cried. "How did you find her, Matthew?"

"Well, without knowing it, I gave Autumn's command in my speech. I said 'push the switch' right before my lamp wouldn't go on. I forgot to turn the lamp off, and it lit up when you gave the command again in your speech. I figured Autumn had to be near the power switch, following the commands."

"Wow, great detective work!" Chris said.

"No, it was good scientific work," Jennifer argued. "Matthew used his observations to form the hypothesis that it was Autumn switching the power off and on."

Maybe Jennifer's right. Maybe I will be a good scientist. Or a detective. I still haven't made up my mind for sure.

PICTURE IT FIRST

By Vashanti Rahaman

It was Friday, glorious Friday, and all was well with Leroy's world. All, that is, except for one single bright orange sheet of paper lurking in his backpack.

Miss Walton always had her weekend assignments printed on bright orange paper. "The better to see them, my dears," she said. "That way you won't come back on Monday and tell me you've lost them." Some teachers have a weird sense of humor.

Actually, Miss Walton was OK, and her orange paper assignments could be fun. But for Leroy there was nothing amusing or entertaining about this one:

Write a story at least two (2) pages long. Include all the words in the list below:

Time Machine	dinosaur
malfunction	volcano
scientist	mouse

If that assignment isn't a weekend killer, I don't know what is, thought Leroy.

Math was unpleasant, but Leroy didn't have any trouble doing it. Science could actually be fun. Social studies was a breeze, with all those maps and charts that he loved to draw.

He really was an "A" student, but even "A" students can have their weak points, and story writing was his. Story writing was something Leroy's mind just refused to tune into.

"Well, you've got to do it," said Mom as she washed the breakfast dishes on Saturday morning. "So you might as well just do it now."

Leroy got out pencils, erasers, and two scribble pads. He sat at the kitchen table and stared at the list of words.

Nothing happened.

There were no flashes of inspiration. No story leaped fully formed into his mind. *What a waste of a good Saturday morning,* thought Leroy.

To tell the truth, it wasn't a particularly good Saturday morning. It was storming outside—rain, wind, thunder, lightning, the whole bit.

Leroy watched sheets of water flowing down the windowpanes. He wondered if the lightning would strike the old hickory tree across the road. He wondered what would happen to the squirrel nest if it did

"Leroy, you've been staring out the window for half an hour," said his mother. "Now, get started!"

She put the potatoes she had been peeling on the stove to boil and wiped her hands. Then she sat down at the table with Leroy and studied the assignment sheet.

"That word list looks as though it has the makings for a good story," she said. "Let's see . . . Time Machine? Who built it? Who's telling the story? . . . Why don't you answer some of those kinds of questions, and see if you get a story idea that way?"

Mom had some pretty goofy ideas sometimes, but occasionally they actually worked. Leroy wrote some answers:

— I tell the story

— Scientist (NOT mad scientist) builds
  the time machine
— goes on trip to the land of dinosaurs
— I go, too!
— most of story takes place at a volcano

Perhaps there was a story there, but Leroy couldn't see it. He began to doodle at the bottom of the page.

"Take a break," said Mom, "it's almost lunchtime anyway. Maybe you'll think of something later."

After lunch it stopped raining, and Joshua came over to visit.

"How's your story going?" asked Leroy.

"Oh, I finished it last night," said Joshua. "It was a snap. Miss Walton practically told us the story with that word list. Want me to do yours for you?"

"Seriously?" asked Leroy.

"Seriously," said Joshua.

Leroy thought for a minute. Joshua knew how much he hated story writing. Joshua hated social studies almost as much. Besides, Joshua really did write good stories, and he really did write them fast. What was a guy to do with a good offer like that?

"Let's go play catch," said Leroy.

He got his glove and they threw a baseball back and forth for a while. But Leroy missed more balls than he caught. It's hard to keep your mind on things when you have a hard assignment waiting.

"Let's go inside," said Leroy.

"No," said Joshua, "I like it out here. If you bring me some paper and a pencil, though, I'll write your story for you here."

"Great!" said Leroy and ran for the door. Then he stopped with his hand on the doorknob. He coughed a little and scratched his ear and stuck his finger down the side of his sneaker to check for stones. This wasn't going to be easy. Finally, he said, "Thanks, Josh, but I think I'd better tough it out myself. You know . . ."

"Yes, I know," said Joshua. "I didn't let Dad do my social studies chart last week either. Take care, Roy. See you later."

Leroy went inside and got out the assignment sheet and the list he had made. *Tough it out is right*, he thought. *I hate this, I hate this, I hate this*. He pounded the table.

Just as he raised his fist for the last pound, he noticed his doodles at the bottom of the page . . . *It's worth a try anyway*, he thought.

Leroy hurried to his room and came back armed with drawing paper and colored markers. For almost an hour he covered page after page with drawings.

"What are you doing?" asked his mother. "I thought you had a story to write. Why are you drawing?"

"But Mom," said Leroy, "this *is* my story. Look, I've drawn it all out. Now I can just look at the pictures and tell the story."

Leroy spread his pictures out in order on the kitchen table. He'd even numbered them so he could put them back in order if they got mixed up.

Mom was amazed.

"What a wonderful story!" she said. "I'd have never thought of making the time machine look like a glowing red circle hanging in the air. Oh, look at them getting chased by that dinosaur—and snatched away just in time by the flying creature! Who'd have thought to make the mouse one of those computer control things. What good ideas!"

When Mom bustled off to tell Dad about the pictures, Leroy got out his writing paper. With the pictures in front of him, the words came quickly, tumbling over each other—almost faster than he could write them. Then he had to correct the spelling, make sure the story flowed right, and write out a neat copy.

The assignment really did take all weekend to do, but Leroy didn't mind. Writing a story wasn't that hard after all. He just had to picture it first.

Too Old
for
Bears

By Lloydene L. Cook

T.J. knew what would be inside the box even before he tore off the teddy bear wrapping paper.

His mother beamed at him as he slowly lifted the lid off the box.

"Oh . . . it's a bear," T.J. said, trying not to sound disappointed.

It was a handsome bear, he had to admit, with thick, chocolate-colored fur and shiny golden eyes. But T.J. had too many bears already. His bookshelf was lined with bears. There were more bears in the toy box and others spilled out of his closet. Bears peeked out from under his bed and poked out of his bureau drawers.

His mother had decorated his room with tumbling teddy bears on the wallpaper. There were teddy bear curtains and a matching bedspread. Perched on his pillow were his two oldest bears—an orange one named "Pumpkin" and a thin, flat one named "Pancake." Under the pillow were the teddy bear pajamas that his mother had sewed for him last month.

For every birthday or holiday, T.J. always received at least one new teddy bear—sometimes two or three!

T.J. hated to hurt his mother's feelings but he was nine years old. He was too old for bears!

What T.J. really liked was outer space. When he lay in his bed that night surrounded by bears, T.J. redecorated his room in his imagination. The ceiling would be painted dark, like the night sky. He would stick up glow-in-the-dark stars to represent his favorite constellations. First would be Pegasus, the flying horse, then Aquila, the eagle, and Cygnus, the swan. If he had room, he would also put up Leo, the lion.

T.J. wished that he could take all the teddy bears that crowded his window seat and replace them with a telescope, so he could study the stars before bedtime each night. And instead of bookshelves filled with teddy bears and books about teddy bears, T.J. wanted books about astronomy and models of rockets and space stations that he had built all by himself. On the wall, he wanted a chart showing all the planets in the universe.

T.J. fell asleep dreaming about his new room and wondering how he would ever convince his mother that he was too old for bears.

The next morning, T.J. went down to breakfast filled with determination.

"Good morning, T.J.," his mother said. "Did you sleep well?"

"I guess so," T.J. said, trying to forget the bad dream he'd had of teddy bears chasing him.

"Mom, will you take me shopping today so I can spend my birthday money?" T.J. asked as he poured a bowl of Teddy Bear Crunchies cereal.

"We can go right after you finish eating," his mother said. "I can't wait to show you the new teddy bears that Mr. Whipple just got in at The Bear Boutique. . . ."

T.J. almost choked on a pink marshmallow bear in his Teddy Bear Crunchies. He washed it down with a sip of orange juice, then took a deep breath. It was now or never. . . .

"No, Mom," T.J. said firmly. "I don't want to look at teddy bears. I don't want to spend my money on teddy bears."

His voice suddenly got louder. "I'M NINE YEARS OLD, MOM! I'M TOO OLD FOR BEARS!"

There. He'd finally said it.

T.J. watched his mother's face turn pale then flush bright pink. She cleared her throat nervously as she cleaned up the breakfast dishes.

"Of course you may spend your money on whatever you want, T.J.," she said crisply. "But, I thought you liked bears. . . ."

T.J. gave her one of his famous bear hugs. "I do like bears, Mom. But I like other things, too."

At the shopping center, T.J. bought a small telescope, a model of a rocket, a book on astronomy, and a chart with all the planets in the universe. His mother bought him a new bedspread and matching curtains that were dark blue sprinkled with meteors, comets, and stars.

It took the two of them all afternoon to pack up all the teddy bears to make room for the new things. T.J. decided to give several of the bears to his cousin, Mandy, who was five years old. He filled another box with bears to donate to his school's yard sale. He carefully packed up his very favorite bears to be stored in the attic, where he could visit them anytime he wanted. When he came to his orange bear, Pumpkin, and the thin, flat one named Pancake, he decided to give them a special place of honor on the window seat, next to the telescope.

T.J. and his mother arranged the glow-in-the-dark stars on the ceiling. All his favorites were there: Pegasus, Aquila, Cygnus, and Leo the lion. But the last one was a secret.

"You'll see what it is tonight, when it gets dark," T.J. teased.

At bedtime, his mother came in to say good night. T.J. turned out the light, and they both looked up. "See . . . there where the Big Dipper is?" T.J. pointed. "If you look real close, you'll see it's actually part of a larger constellation called 'The Great Bear.'"

And there it was. A giant teddy bear made of twinkling stars was directly over T.J.'s bed.

"That's there in case I get lonesome for bears," T.J. said with a grin.

Lemonade
and
Lilacs

By Betty Bates

I have a place where I go when I'm angry at somebody who laughed at me.

Or when I want to play my kazoo.

Or when I just want to be quiet and smell the flowers and think.

It's a special, safe place where nobody can find me.

Well, almost nobody.

My place is outside under the lilac trees. There are four of them in a square. With their branches coming together for a roof, they make a house.

Just now after my sister, Sil, made fun of my drawing of a rabbit, I came to my special place. I sat against the trunk of a lilac tree, talking out loud and saying all the things I wished I'd said to her. "You don't have to be so nasty," I growled at a spider spinning a web. "Bet you couldn't draw a rabbit any better than I did."

The spider didn't answer. It didn't seem to care. Nobody seemed to care.

"Hi."

I turned around. There stood Grandma, holding two paper cups.

"Grandma! How did you find me? This is my secret place "

"Sweetheart," said Grandma, "I've known about this place for fifty years."

Fifty years! How dare she?

She ducked under a branch and sat next to me holding the cups carefully. "You don't need to stare," she said. "I brought you something cool to drink."

I took a cup.

"You might say 'thank you,'" she said.

"Thank you." It was lemonade. My favorite I gulped some down But how could she know about this place? It's my place and nobody else's.

"When I was your age, I used to come here," she said. "It was my special place. My little house."

Her house?

"I came," she went on, "whenever I was angry at somebody, or when I wanted to play a tune on a blade of grass, or when I just wanted to be quiet and think. Sometimes I drank lemonade here."

The lemonade wasn't a bad idea.

"You mean these lilac trees were here then?"

"Yes, with the sun shining through the leaves making patterns on the ground, just the way it does now."

"But that was an awfully long time ago."

"It doesn't seem so long ago." She set her cup down and snuck her arm around me. "I promise I won't tell anyone about this place."

I snuggled close to her. "Sib laughed at me."

"I know. I don't think she meant to be mean I think she'll want to make up."

Maybe.

After I finished my lemonade, I might go and talk with Sib. I might.

And how could I be upset with Grandma? After all, she got here first. And I knew she'd keep my secret. Our secret

"I'm sorry I disturbed you," she said.

"It's OK. Come any time."

"No, thanks." She got to her feet. "I have to go now, and I won t come back again. But maybe someday, years from now, someone else will be sitting here, and you'll bring the lemonade."

I couldn't imagine that would ever happen.

Would it?

I felt better. I'd go and talk with Sib, for sure.

After I finished my lemonade.

Sadie's Sparkle

By Lloydene Cook

Sadie was the youngest child in a family with lots of sparkle.

Her papa was the Triple County Hog Calling Champion.

Her mama sewed beautiful prize-winning patchwork quilts.

Her brother, Buster, could stand on his head, wiggle his ears, and whistle "Dixie" backward.

And her sister, Clorissa, could sing better than a meadowlark on a sunny morning in May.

The thing Sadie liked to do best was make up stories in her head, but she was too shy to share them with anyone.

One summer afternoon, Sadie sat on the porch step watching a doodlebug dig tunnels in the soft, red dirt. With her bare toe, Sadie dug a tunnel too, but her tunnel collapsed.

Grandma looked up from the pan of butterbeans she was shelling.

"What's troubling you, Sadie?"

"Everybody does things better than I do," Sadie sighed. "Even an old doodlebug!"

"I reckon you haven't found your gift yet," Grandma said.

"What gift is that?" Sadie asked.

"Everybody has a gift," Grandma explained. "Something that makes you sparkle. You haven't found your sparkle yet."

"How do I find my sparkle?" Sadie asked.

"Look inside yourself," Grandma said.

"And how will I know if I find it?"

"You will feel special all over," Grandma said.

So for the rest of the week Sadie looked. She sang songs with Clorissa, and she whittled with Grandpa. She sewed with Mama, and she baked peach pies with Grandma.

But still Sadie had no sparkle.

One night after supper the family gathered on the porch to watch the sun go down.

Mama was busy quilting, Papa was rocking, Grandma was peeling peaches, and Grandpa was whittling a toy alligator. Off in the yard, Clorissa was singing a new song, and Buster was standing on his head.

Grandma put down her paring knife. With a far-away look in her eyes, she said, "I remember how my mama used to tell me stories on nights like this—best stories I ever heard."

The only sound on the soft night air was the chirping of crickets.

Finally, Sadie said very quietly, "I know a story, Grandma . . .

"Far back in Deep Mossy Swamp, there lives a big old hairy monster all covered with moss. He's so big that frogs live in his ears. Every night at sundown he comes out of the swamp looking for something to eat."

As Sadie told her story, everyone stopped to listen. Clorissa and Buster sat down beside Sadie. The monster seemed to be close by.

"People tried setting traps to catch the monster, but he always escaped into the swamp. When they tried to follow his footprints, those folks disappeared and were never heard from again.

"And they never have caught him," Sadie concluded. "Some folks say he's still wandering in these woods at night, hungry for his supper!"

Buster shivered. "That was a good story."

"Tell us another one. Please!" Clorissa begged.

Sadie tingled all over. She felt sure she must be sparkling as bright as a lightning bug. She smiled at Grandma.

"Once upon a time . . . "

Things That Go "BOCK" in the Night

By Vashanti Rahaman

Sally was a little scared. A new class would be bad enough, but this was a new class in a new school in a new town. Perhaps Sally was brave to be only a little scared, but she did not feel very brave at all.

When she went with Mom to see her new school she felt a little better. Everything seemed all right—well, almost everything.

The kids seemed all right. So did the playground and her new teacher. Most of the stuff in her new classroom was all right, too.

But the Humpty Dumpty doll was all wrong. It was too babyish. After all, this wasn't a kinder·garten or first-grade classroom. And to make matters worse, it hung from the ceiling right over Sally's new desk. What if it fell from up there right onto her head? Anything could happen in a strange school.

Sally worried about the Humpty Dumpty doll all the way home. She worried about it all evening. Just before bedtime she asked, "What was that Humpty Dumpty doll made of?"

"What Humpty Dumpty doll?" asked Mom.

"The one right in the middle of the classroom," said Sally.

"Oh, that one," said Mom. "Maybe it was a soft stuffed toy."

"No, I don't think so," said Sally. "It looked like it was painted or something."

"Maybe it was wood," said Dad.

"Maybe it was a clay pot sort of thing," said Mom.

"Maybe," said Sally uncomfortably. Getting clunked on the head by a chunk of wood or a clay pot would hurt!

Later that night Sally woke up screaming. She huddled under her blanket, too scared to peep out.

"What was it, dear?" asked Mom, as she came into Sally's room.

"Was it a bad dream?" asked Dad.

Sally just snuggled close to Mom. It was no use telling Mom and Dad about her dream. They'd probably think it was funny.

It was that Humpty Dumpty doll, of course. In her dream he had chased her down the school hallway. She could hear him bumping along, *bock, bock, bock*, behind her.

Mom and Dad went back to their room and Sally tried to sleep again. She had just dozed off when she heard it again, *bock, bock, bock*. Sally sat up and listened. Then she got out of bed.

The noise was coming from the living room. It seemed louder now, and there was a sort of hum, too, *Humm . . . bock, bock, bock*.

Sally shut her eyes and clenched her fists. "Dear God," she whispered, "are you awake? I need some company. I don't like my new town or my new school or my new house. I feel all alone and afraid. I'm afraid Mom and Dad will laugh and tell me not to be such a baby if I call them again. But You know how I feel. You won't laugh."

Then she opened her eyes a little and slowly looked around her. Would God answer? Would it be scary if He did?

All she could hear was *Humm . . . bock, bock, bock*, and Dad's snoring.

Sally gathered all her courage and went into the living room. The noise was really loud now. Quickly, she turned on the lights . . . and found herself staring at the fan on the ceiling.

What a disappointment . . . and a relief!

The fan turned slowly to the right, then it turned slowly to the left, then it went *bock, bock, bock*.

Sally went back to bed. "Thank you, God," she whispered as she drifted off to sleep.

The next day Sally asked her new teacher what the Humpty Dumpty doll was made of.

"See for yourself," said the teacher, as she took the doll down.

It was like a paper balloon—as harmless and as light as a blown-up paper bag.

"We made it last month, before you came," said the teacher. "It's just scrap paper glued onto a balloon. And we painted it, of course."

"We could show you how to make it," said one of Sally's classmates.

"Great!" said Sally. "I'd like that."

That night Sally had another "*bock, bock, bock*" dream. The Humpty Dumpty doll was chasing her again.

"You can't scare me," she shouted over her shoulder in her dream. "It's just the fan making that noise."

Then she turned around and saw that the doll was getting blown around by a fan. Her new classmates were trying to catch it and having great fun. What a dream!

Sally laughed out loud in her sleep and woke herself up. She turned her pillow over to the cool side, pulled up her blanket, and smiled to herself in the darkness. Maybe a new class in a new school wouldn't be so bad after all. Then she went back to sleep feeling very brave indeed.

Carmen
and the
Kidnapped
Pumpkins

By Marianne Mitchell

"Aren't they the most beautiful orange babies you ever saw, Grandpa?" Ten-year-old Carmen poked her dirt-covered hands into her pockets.

"Yep, sure are. Best ever," said Grandpa.

As Carmen walked around her garden, dried leaves crunched like cornflakes under her feet. Soon it would be Halloween, and she would have to cut her pumpkins from the vines and take them to the market.

Carmen and her grandfather had a small plot of land in the city's community garden lot. Here they had grown beans, tomatoes, squash, and beets. Now, as chilly weather arrived, the last crop was ready to harvest.

Carmen gazed at the other small gardens, now abandoned for the winter. What fun it had been this summer to swap gardening tips with everyone! Some folks had grown as many as four hundred tomato plants in their little spaces. But the garden right next to Carmen hadn't produced a thing. Only weeds.

"Why didn't Lucas take care of his garden, Grandpa?" Carmen asked.

"Didn't know how, I guess." Grandpa reached down and yanked a big weed. "A good gardener never gives up. You take care of your plants, and they give you something in return. Your hard work, Carmen, gave you a dozen beautiful pumpkins. They'll each make a fine jack-o'-lantern."

It was easy for Carmen to imagine faces on her pumpkins. She had even given her little family names. The one with the yellow patch was called "Goldy." The one with the wrinkled skin she called "Crinkles." The biggest one she called "Grande." There was even a pumpkin that reminded her of her little sister, so she called it "Lupita."

"I really wish I didn't have to give them up," sighed Carmen.

"Now remember, you grew them to sell," said Grandpa. "That's what all the digging and fussing was about."

"I know, I know," said Carmen. "I'm just going to miss my big orange babies!"

"Well, say 'good night' to your babies. It's suppertime, and I bet you have homework to do."

Carmen blew her pumpkins a kiss. "Now, sleep tight, everybody!"

When Carmen and Grandpa returned the next day, a terrible sight greeted them. The snaky vines were bare, with nothing left but the stems. Someone had kidnapped Carmen's pumpkins!

"Grandpa! Where are they?" gasped Carmen. Her big, brown eyes filled with tears.

"Looks like someone wanted your pumpkins real bad," Grandpa said.

"It's not fair!" she sobbed. "After all our work!" She stared at the empty vines in disbelief. "Let's go to the farmers' market right now. Maybe we'll find the thief there. And my pumpkins!"

"You can't just go up and accuse someone," Grandpa said. "You'll have to have proof."

"I'll have proof. Let me get a sack and some things from the garden. Then we'll go."

Soon Carmen and Grandpa were walking the aisles of the huge open-air market. There were tons of vegetables for sale—squash, corn, beans, and pumpkins. Mountains of pumpkins! Carmen was surprised there were so many piles to check out. She stopped and examined each pile slowly before moving on to the next one. Finally, she saw a little group of twelve very familiar-looking pumpkins.

"There they are! Those are my pumpkins! See, there's Goldy, and Grande, and Crinkles. And that one is Lupita."

"Young man, are these your pumpkins?" Grandpa asked the boy who was making a FOR SALE sign. When the boy looked up, they saw it was Lucas, owner of the weedy garden.

"Yeah, they're mine." Lucas went back to work on his sign.

"Oh no, these are my pumpkins!" shouted Carmen. "You stole them from our garden last night."

"You can't prove that," mumbled Lucas, trying not to meet her angry stare.

"I'd know my pumpkins anywhere, and these are mine!" Carmen wagged her finger at Lucas.

Grandpa patted Carmen's shoulder, trying to calm her.

"They look like your pumpkins, Carmen, but can you prove it?"

"I sure can!" said Carmen. "When something gets broken, you fix it by matching the pieces together, right? Well, in this sack I have the pieces that match my pumpkins."

She opened her sack and dumped it out. Fresh cut stems spilled out all over the ground. Carmen sat down and began to match each stem to a pumpkin.

"Look! See how this stem matches this pumpkin? And this one fits that one over there. And this one goes to Goldy. And this one fits Crinkles. . . . "

Lucas grew restless as Carmen matched stem after stem. Slowly, he started to back away, ready to run.

One look from Grandpa stopped him cold. "Well, where did you get these pumpkins?"

Lucas stared at the ground. "Her garden was always full of things. I couldn't grow anything. Not even a stupid pumpkin."

"You didn't have to steal them! We would have helped you, right Grandpa?"

"All you had to do was ask, Lucas. In fact, we could become real pests with all our advice."

Lucas ran his hand across the pumpkins. "It looked so easy. Seeds in, pumpkins up. I guess you're pretty angry, huh?"

"I'd feel a lot better if you'd help me sell these pumpkins today," said Carmen. "Then we can start planning for next year."

"Next year?" asked Lucas.

"Sure. You don't want to grow weeds again, do you?"

Lucas flashed her a smile and picked up the FOR SALE sign. Before long they had sold every pumpkin but one.

Carmen kept Grande for her jack-o'-lantern. That night, she and Lucas scooped out the seeds and divided them. Lucas looked at his seeds and wondered what magic they held. Carmen knew. She could almost imagine the faces of her next family of big orange babies.

Old Blue

By Darleen Bailey Beard

Old Blue couldn't believe it. His family was selling him! He glanced at his owner's son, Rupert T. Riley. Rupert looked shocked.

"Here's something to remember me by," Rupert cried, hiding his lucky marble in Old Blue's hubcap. "I made an A in math with this. Maybe you'll have good luck, too."

Old Blue drove out the driveway and down the street with his new owner, Mr. Rodriguez. He wondered if he would ever see Rupert's smile again.

Good-bye, Rupert, Old Blue thought. *I'll never forget you.*

Every sunrise, Mr. Rodriguez drove Old Blue to the ocean. Old Blue watched him set up his canvas, then brush on gobs of green and splotches of red to create the most beautiful paintings Old Blue had ever seen.

Mr. Rodriguez painted a seashell on each of Old Blue's doors. The artist became world renowned for his dazzling seascapes. The Art Society presented him with an official Society dune buggy.

From then on, Mr. Rodriguez gadded about the beach in his Society buggy, never giving Old Blue a second glance.

Old Blue was left in the sand with the sun scorching his roof.

When Mr. Rodriguez gave Old Blue to his brother-in-law, Chef Pierre, Old Blue was glad.

"Each shell was hand-painted by me, the world's *greatest* artist!" Mr. Rodriguez bragged. "But I'm too rich and famous to be seen driving a car with such a rattle."

Chef Pierre drove Old Blue to Chef's Market. Through the market door, Old Blue gazed in amazement as Chef Pierre dipped frozen bananas in chocolate, sprinkled cookies with raspberry drops, and spooned butterscotch pudding into cream puffs. But Chef Pierre ate nearly as much as he sold. So he put a refrigerator in the back of Old Blue.

Soon the chef's belly grew so large, he couldn't fit behind Old Blue's steering wheel. The only thing he could fit into was a bus. So he sold Old Blue to Freddy Knotready.

Freddy was always late and hurried through red lights, stop signs, and even roadblocks.

Freddy wasn't only late going places, but also late mailing his house payments. When the bank repossessed his home, he made Old Blue pull a trailer for him and his family to live in.

Freddy didn't change Old Blue's oil. He let his seven children jump on the seats. He remembered to put in gas only after it was too late.

When Freddy fell behind on his car payments, the bank took Old Blue away.

"This is a real road runner!" Freddy told the banker. "I meant to find out where that rattle is, but it's too late now. Maybe you can figure it out."

The bank sold Old Blue to Dr. Seebetter, its nicest customer. She drove Old Blue to her office.

Through the bay window, Old Blue watched the doctor examine eyes and fit contact lenses.

One day, Dr. Seebetter didn't wear her glasses. While backing out of her parking space, she knocked over a light post. Old Blue's fender bent and twisted.

Dr. Seebetter traded him and two free eye exams for a new car.

Doesn't anyone want me? Old Blue thought.

Day after day, Old Blue sat in Honest John's Car Lot. Week after week, Honest John lowered the price in Old Blue's window.

But no one wanted Old Blue.

His lights weren't as bright as they once were. His tires were almost bald. The metal under his paint was beginning to show.

Finally, as Old Blue was about to be driven to the junkyard, a teenager came onto the lot.

"This car reminds me of one we had when I was a kid," the young man said, looking through Old Blue's window. "But our car didn't have seashells painted on each door. It didn't have a refrigerator in the back seat, a trailer hitch, or a bent fender, either. This couldn't be Old Blue."

Old Blue lifted his headlights. He hadn't heard that name in a long time. There, standing in front of him, was Rupert T. Riley!

"Rupert, Rupert," he choked, trying to start his engine. "It's *me*! Old Blue!"

He tried to wave his doors, but all of them were locked.

He tried to honk his horn, but his honker wouldn't work.

If he didn't think of *something*, Rupert would go away.

"Old Blue was a gem," Rupert told Honest John.

"So is this one," Honest John said, kicking a front tire. "It has a small rattle, but it's a good old car."

That's it! Old Blue thought. He knew exactly what he had to do.

With all his might, he held his exhaust, and off popped his front hubcap. It spun around in circles and landed at Rupert's feet.

Rupert bent down. "I can't believe it!" he said, picking up the marble. "This *is* Old Blue!"

"I don't understand," Honest John said.

"See this marble? This was *my* marble," Rupert said. "I hid it in Old Blue's hubcap for good luck."

"Does this mean you want to buy the car?" Honest John asked.

"*Do* I?" Rupert said, getting in.

Old Blue was so excited to have Rupert back, he sped through the parking lot, leaped into the air, and popped a wheelie!

"Well, Old Blue," Rupert said, patting the dash. "It's great to have you back again. All you need is a little mending and a new coat of paint. I think red is *definitely* the color for you!"

A Pretty Christmas for Ivy

By Diane L. Burns

Birdie opened the porch door wide to whisper to Mama, who rocked a sleeping Ivy inside on the hearth. "I dug up the tree I wanted, Mama, but I had to stuff it into the canning kettle to keep it from tipping over." She lugged the pot into the doorway. "Look at it, Mama—the tree is skimpier than I remembered; it leans something awful."

"No matter, Birdie," Mama consoled her. "It will still be a pretty surprise for your sister'

Birdie studied the spindly evergreen and thought of past Christmas trees: fat and fragrant, with popcorn chains and shiny glass balls and candles dripping perfumed wax. Those beautiful Christmases had been left behind in Boston when they'd sold everything to pay for Ivy's doctor bills and moved to this healthier place. Here in Cedar Hollow, folks made whatever they needed, even at Christmastime.

As if she were reading Birdie's thoughts, Mama said gently, "The shape of the tree won't matter much to Ivy. Remember, child: 'Beauty is in the eye of the beholder.'"

But that was exactly the trouble. Not even sweet Ivy could possibly like such a crooked, homely tree as this one. It hadn't looked so awful out in the pasture, framed by snow; but now, here on the porch, the gap-branched evergreen looked like a person too weak to stand up straight. The way Ivy had been before they'd moved away from the city air to the purer air of Mama's Blue Ridge Mountains.

Or maybe . . . Birdie sighed. Maybe this tree felt ashamed to be crammed into a kettle. Birdie sighed again. Even if she had miles of popcorn chain and hundreds of glass ornaments, she couldn't help this tree. It would have been better left in the pasture where Ivy could be taken to see it. But Ivy was still too weak to go outdoors. Oh, why had she promised Ivy a pretty Christmas?

Birdie turned from the tree, swallowing hard. Just beyond the porch, Cedar Creek's sandy bank sparkled in frosty December sunshine. Slender grasses swayed like ribbons, and rose hips clung in crimson clumps from the bushes. Even a mound of leftover coal dust glittered near the porch steps. All together, it was a lovely picture. It wasn't fair that such pretty sights were meant to stay outdoors.

"If only I could bring the prettiness from the outside to the inside places," Birdie muttered, "and make it all stick like glue."

What a foolish thought. Or was it? Birdie pulled in a sharp little breath. Oh maybe, just maybe, she *could* stick some of the prettiness inside . . .

Birdie slipped into the cabin. "Mama, can you spare a little flour?" she asked hopefully. "It's for the tree."

Rocking quietly, Mama nodded.

In a bowl, Birdie mixed flour and some water into a smooth paste. Buttoning her sweater against the chill and grabbing the bowl of paste, she darted into the yard. Soon, she was back with an armload of treasures to lay on the table.

"Good, Ivy's still asleep. Please don't let her wake up yet," Birdie whispered to Mama.

Dutifully, Mama rocked and rocked, humming lullabies while Birdie pulled the potted evergreen inside. Ivy slept on as Birdie moved quickly between the table and the tree. Afternoon shadows on the mountain lengthened into twilight. The fire in the grate sighed as it settled, tucking warmth into every corner of the cabin. And still Ivy slept.

Finally, Birdie announced, "Ready!"

Mama nudged Ivy awake to discover the pretty Christmas tree. In the firelight, she saw slender grasses hung everywhere from the tree's branches, crusted with a shimmery glue-coat of paste and creek sand. Glued coal dust edged the evergreen's pinecones. Red rose hips bobbed here and there, filling any gaps with bold bits of Christmas color.

Toasty-warm air wavered around the fireplace, tickling the tree. The branches swayed gently and the tip nodded. The hunched tree shimmered and trembled all over.

Ivy clapped her hands. "Look, Mama," she chirped, her thin face bright with pleasure, "the pretty tree is dancing. Oh, it's dancing!"

Birdie knelt beside the rocker and rested her head on Mama's shoulder. "None of our Christmas trees in Boston ever danced, did they, Mama?" she asked, looking in wonder at the tree.

"No," said Mama, cuddling Ivy and smiling at Birdie, "they never did."